this book belongs to

Miss Violet's Shining Day

Miss Violet's Shining Day

STORY AND PICTURES BY
JANE BRESKIN ZALBEN

Boyds Mills Press

I wish to thank Jane Yolen, a friend of twenty years, and Pam Conrad, who both read it first, believing in the story; to Ann K. Beneduce and Sandra Jordan, my old editors, who don't know it—but they were the source of inspiration; to Jan Keen, my new editor, for her enthusiasm; and to my son Jonathan Zalben, who fills my heart with music. I especially want to thank Sniffles Zalben, my model, who gives the best rabbit kisses and hugs in the whole world, and to Marilyn E. Marlow, for everything.

Published by Caroline House / Boyds Mills Press, Inc.
A Highlights Company
815 Church Street / Honesdale, Pennsylvania 18431
Printed in Mexico

Publisher Cataloging-in-Publication Data
Zalben, Jane Breskin.
Miss Violet's shining day / story and pictures by Jane Breskin Zalben.—1st ed. [32]p. : col. ill. ; cm.
Summary : Miss Violet's humdrum days come to life when she learns how to play the trombone.
1. Musical instruments—Juvenile fiction. 2. Picture books for children.
[1. Musical instruments—Fiction.] I. Title. [E]—dc20 1995
Library of Congress Catalog Card Number 94-70687
ISBN 1-56397-234-4

First edition, 1995
Book designed by Jane Breskin Zalben
The text of this book was set in Palatino.
The illustrations were done in watercolor with a tiny brush.
Distributed by St. Martin's Press
10 9 8 7 6 5 4 3 2 1

To my family, with all my love,
who understand I need art and writing
like breathing air

$\mathcal{M}$iss Violet led an ordinary life. She got up in the quiet of each morning, went to work in a button factory, came home, and sipped a cup of hot tea. At night she would curl up with a book in an old worn armchair and fall asleep. Her house was still, except for a ticking clock and the thump of a wisteria branch against a windowpane.

Weekends, she went for walks in the country, collecting colored pebbles and wildflowers. For lunch she would eat a stalk of celery and alfalfa sprouts. On special occasions she would have a crisp carrot, fresh strawberries, and endive.

One day Miss Violet passed Sir Reginald Dewlap's house, a house she had passed for years on her way home from the factory. She heard something unusual. Loud. Bright. Brassy. Before Miss Violet could think, she found herself flying up the path to Sir Dewlap's. With all her courage, she tapped on the front door.

"Come in, come in," Sir Dewlap boomed.
Miss Violet stared down at the path. "My name is —"
"Miss Violet, yes, yes, do come in," he urged.
"I was wondering," she paused, "was that you playing?"
Sir Dewlap wiped his whiskers and nodded,
fingering the frayed buttons on his vest.

"A cousin who will be traveling the far seas
for many years gave me his trombone.
I'll play a piece just for you," he said.
Miss Violet swayed to the rhythm with each slide
of the trombone until the last note faded away.
She felt all warm inside. There was a feeling
that she needed music, like breathing air,
and somehow Sir Dewlap understood.

"Would you like to try?" he asked. "I'll teach you."
Miss Violet picked up the trombone and placed the
mouthpiece to her lips. She took a deep breath and
blew. Her heart raced when sound came out. A-flats
sounded breezy to her ears. She spent the whole
afternoon just trying to play.

Her first lesson began the following day.
She played the next, and the next, and every
chance she got, practicing in the hayloft of
Sir Reginald's barn. Sometimes Miss Violet
played until dawn.

Now Miss Violet hummed on her way to work, smiling at neighbors. Where she had always been careful at her job in the button factory, purple buttons got into boxes labeled 'blue' or 'green.' And round ones into square. And wooden into plastic.

As time went by, all Miss Violet could think about was music. One evening, she noticed a sign on Mr. Timothy Hay's feed store:

Town Hall Concert

AUDITIONS HELD SATURDAY MORNING.

PROMPTLY 10 A.M.

See Concertmaster Christopher Lapin

The day of the auditions, Miss Violet passed by Town Hall.
Madame Nicole belted out an aria from the opera *Aïda*.
Her children performed their major scales on the violin.
Mr. Hay's clerk sang themes from several Broadway shows,
while the entire local elementary school tap-danced.
And the Bee Bop De Bop Jazz Band was doing the blues.
Miss Violet thumped to the beat. She wanted to join in,
but she was too scared to perform. She left, sadly.

Weeks later, on the evening of the musicale,
everyone dressed in their finest clothes.
But not Miss Violet. She went to the hayloft.
And played. And played. And played.
Her trills vibrated. Her glissandos baroomped.
Her slurs streamed, and her tones tingled.
Sound echoed throughout the countryside.
Where was that music coming from?
Who was playing it? The neighbors wondered.
And searched. Finding no one.

WESTBORO LRC

Finally the loudest note Miss Violet had ever reached echoed in the barn and throughout the village. Miss Violet scooped up the trombone and carried it over bumpy fields and rocky hills, falling into a stream.

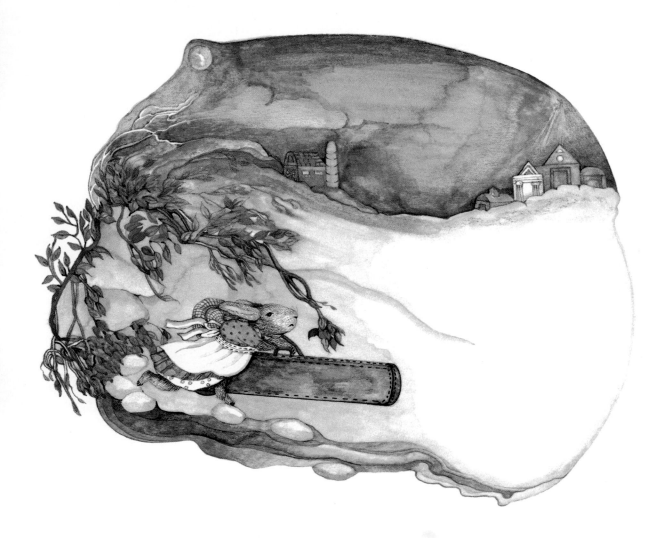

Wet and tired, she burst into Town Hall to a sudden hush.
Miss Violet paused, catching her breath, and then played
the piece she had been practicing with Sir Dewlap for months.

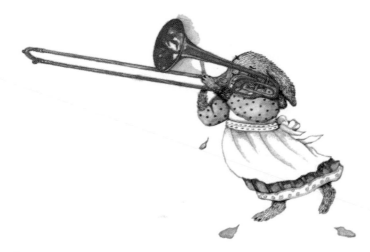

When Miss Violet blew the last note, everyone clapped.
There were thunderous "bravos" and "encores."
Sir Reginald Dewlap smiled proudly. "Bravo!" he cried.
"Oh, Sir Dewlap," Miss Violet whispered,
"how can I ever thank you?"
Sir Dewlap patted his chest.
"Find me some new buttons."

The following day, Miss Violet visited her friend. "This is for you. It isn't much," Miss Violet said, placing a gold button in his palm. A musical note was painted in the center with the initials R. D. Sir Dewlap tapped the trombone. "This is yours."

"I couldn't," Miss Violet gasped.

"You could! You make beautiful music."

"*You* make beautiful music," she said.

"We do," he added.

"Together," she agreed happily.

The concertmaster invited Miss Violet to play
in next year's concert as *the* guest performer.
Miss Violet performed every year thereafter,
except the year she took her band—
Miss V and the Wild Alfalfas—on the road
to the Cottontail Club.
She no longer felt shy. She had new friends.
Her music. She loved her bright, yellow,
brassy trombone. And life.